W9-BAI-421

The Mystery of the Backdoor Bundle

THREE COUSINS DETECTIVE CLUB®

#1 / The Mystery of the White Elephant
#2 / The Mystery of the Silent Nightingale
#3 / The Mystery of the Wrong Dog
#4 / The Mystery of the Dancing Angels
#5 / The Mystery of the Hobo's Message
#6 / The Mystery of the Magi's Treasure
#7 / The Mystery of the Haunted Lighthouse
#8 / The Mystery of the Dolphin Detective
#9 / The Mystery of the Eagle Feather
#10 / The Mystery of the Silly Goose
#11 / The Mystery of the Copycat Clown
#12 / The Mystery of the Honeybees' Secret
#13 / The Mystery of the Gingerbread House
#14 / The Mystery of the Zoo Camp
#15 / The Mystery of the Goldfish Pond
#16 / The Mystery of the Traveling Button
#17 / The Mystery of the Birthday Party
#18 / The Mystery of the Lost Island
#19 / The Mystery of the Wedding Cake
#20 / The Mystery of the Sand Castle
#21 / The Mystery of the Sock Monkeys
#22 / The Mystery of the African Gray
#23 / The Mystery of the Butterfly Garden
#24 / The Mystery of the Book Fair
#25 / The Mystery of the Coon Cat
#26 / The Mystery of the Runaway Scarecrow
#27 / The Mystery of the Attic Lion
#28 / The Mystery of the Backdoor Bundle

The Mystery of the Backdoor Bundle

Elspeth Campbell Murphy
Illustrated by Joe Nordstrom

BETHANY HOUSE PUBLISHERS
MINNEAPOLIS, MINNESOTA 55438

The Mystery of the Backdoor Bundle
Copyright © 2000
Elspeth Campbell Murphy

Cover and story illustrations by Joe Nordstrom
Cover design by Lookout Design Group, Inc.

Scripture quotation is from the HOLY BIBLE, NEW
INTERNATIONAL VERSION®. Copyright © 1973, 1978, 1984
by International Bible Society. Used by permission of Zondervan
Publishing House. All rights reserved. The "NIV" and "New
International Version" trademarks are registered in the United
States Patent and Trademark Office by International Bible Society.
Use of either trademark requires the permission of International
Bible Society.

All rights reserved. No part of this publication may be reproduced,
stored in a retrieval system, or transmitted in any form or by any
means—electronic, mechanical, photocopying, recording, or
otherwise—without the prior written permission of the publisher
and copyright owners.

Published by Bethany House Publishers
A Ministry of Bethany Fellowship International
11400 Hampshire Avenue South
Minneapolis, Minnesota 55438
www.bethanyhouse.com

Printed in the United States of America by
Bethany Press International, Minneapolis, Minnesota 55438

Library of Congress Cataloging-in-Publication Data

CIP data applied for

ISBN 0–7642–2136–1   CIP

3.99

ELSPETH CAMPBELL MURPHY has been a familiar name in Christian publishing for over twenty years, with more than one hundred books to her credit and sales approaching six million worldwide. She is the author of the bestselling series *David and I Talk to God* and *The Kids From Apple Street Church,* as well as the 1990 Gold Medallion winner *Do You See Me, God?,* and two books of prayer meditations for teachers, *Chalkdust* and *Recess.* A graduate of Trinity College and Moody Bible Institute, Elspeth and her husband, Mike, make their home in Chicago, where she writes full time.

Contents

*"[The Lord] heals the brokenhearted
and binds up their wounds."*

Psalm 147:3

Spider

*I*n Sarah-Jane Cooper's opinion, Lee Marley did not look like the kind of person who could fix dolls.

With his black jeans and black sweater and black jacket and black hair, he looked like his nickname—Spider.

Spider looked like the kind of person who could fix motorcycles—which he could.

But he was also good at sewing. So good, in fact, that Sarah-Jane's mother had hired him to be her assistant. She had a small sewing and decorating business.

One day a customer asked if they could repair an old doll. And it turned out Spider knew how to do that, too.

He did such a good job that more and more

people brought in dolls for repair. And before they knew it, Spider and Sarah-Jane's mother were running a little doll hospital.

Sarah-Jane was impressed.

She loved dolls and had quite a collection herself. Relatives had been giving them to her for birthdays and Christmas ever since she was a baby. And now there was almost no space left in her room for her.

Still, she wouldn't have it any other way.

Whenever Sarah-Jane's cousins Timothy Dawson and Titus McKay visited, they gave her a hard time about her dolls.

They were doing it again this morning.

"Boys have dolls, too," Sarah-Jane replied. "Except you guys call them 'action figures.'"

"Ha!" Timothy and Titus exclaimed.

It was the same conversation they'd had word for word many times before. And it seemed that "Ha!" was the only snappy response the boys could ever come up with.

Sarah-Jane found that very satisfying.

And now there was the doll hospital.

That put Timothy and Titus in an awkward position. They positively *loved* hanging out with Spider. He had given them rides on his motorcycle, so the boys were his pals for life. But in order to hang out with Spider, they had to hang out with sewing machines and bolts of fabric.

And now dolls. Where would it all end?

Sarah-Jane smiled sweetly at them. "Spider's working today. Would you like to go up to the doll hospital and say hello?"

But before the boys could answer, there came a loud knock at the kitchen door.

2

Funny Weird

*T*he cousins jumped and looked at one another in surprise.

No one ever came to the back door. Visitors came to the front door.

Customers came to the side door. The side door was at the top of the outside stairway that led up to the office-workroom.

So who could *this* be?

Sarah-Jane tiptoed to the window and peeked out.

"That's funny," she said.

"Funny ha-ha or funny weird?" asked Titus.

"Funny weird," replied Sarah-Jane.

"What's funny weird?" asked Timothy.

Sarah-Jane shrugged and tried to sound ca-

sual about it when she said, "There's no one there."

"What do you mean, there's no one there?" asked Titus.

"Just what I said," replied Sarah-Jane. "There's no one there."

"There has to be someone there," said Timothy. "*Somebody* knocked. It couldn't have been the wind."

"There's no one there," repeated Sarah-Jane.

This was maybe not the most intelligent

conversation they had ever had. But they were all a little spooked, and no one wanted to admit it.

"It's probably nothing," said Titus. "It's probably just someone playing a dumb joke. You know, like kids who ring doorbells and run away."

"In that case," said Sarah-Jane. "Maybe they're still hanging around and we can see who it is and catch them."

This made them feel better.

A mystery to solve.

The three cousins had a detective club, and solving mysteries was their favorite thing to do.

Together the three of them went to the door. And on the count of three, Sarah-Jane pulled it open.

They were met by a blast of cold, damp wind.

Quickly they glanced around, but they saw nothing and no one.

They were just about to close the door and try to forget the whole thing when they happened to look down.

Something had been left on the doorstep.

3

The Mysterious Bundle

The "something" was a small basket. Inside the basket was something bundled up in a baby blanket.

"Oh!" cried Sarah-Jane. "I bet it's a foundling!"

"A *what*?!" said Timothy and Titus together.

Sarah-Jane had read a lot of fairy tales, and this was a word she had picked up from her reading.

"A *foundling*," she repeated. "You know, a baby left on the doorstep where you don't know who its parents are. Sometimes it's even a baby princess. Or a prince. Like Moses."

Sarah-Jane had read a lot of Bible stories, too. Timothy and Titus stared at her.

Sarah-Jane had seen that look before. It meant: Our cousin has lost her mind.

"S-J!" said Titus in some alarm. "You don't mean to tell us that there's a *baby* in there, do you?"

Sarah-Jane knew that she had a tendency to let her imagination run away with her.

And she knew that this was probably one of those times.

She bent down, picked up the basket, and closed the door against the cold.

"It's not heavy enough to be a baby," she said.

"Then what is it?" asked Timothy.

There was only one way to find out.

Sarah-Jane set the basket on the table and gently pulled back the blanket.

At the same moment, all three cousins gasped and jumped back.

Because—it really *was* a baby in a basket!

Or at least that's what they thought for one split second.

"A doll!" gulped Timothy.

Titus clapped his hand over his chest. "It's just a doll!"

In Sarah-Jane's opinion, it wasn't "just a

doll" at all. It was the most wonderful thing she had ever seen.

"Oooh!" cried Sarah-Jane, lifting the doll carefully from the covers. "Isn't she *adorable*?"

Timothy and Titus shrugged as if to say, "How would we know?"

"Well, she is," said Sarah-Jane firmly. "She's just adorable. She doesn't look as if she came from a store. She looks as if someone made her all by hand. Maybe a long time ago. Maybe she's almost a hundred years old!"

Timothy and Titus shrugged again as if to say, "We couldn't care less."

But curiosity got the better of them.

It always did.

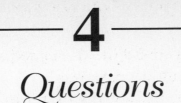

Questions

*T*imothy took the doll from Sarah-Jane and looked at it closely.

The doll had a cloth body, and she was dressed in old-fashioned clothes. Her dark hair and beautiful face had been painted on.

Timothy, who was very good at art, was impressed in spite of himself.

Sarah-Jane could tell.

Then Titus took the doll from Timothy and looked at her closely.

He shook his head, puzzled. "I don't know. She looks in pretty good shape to me. Some wear and tear, of course. But what would you expect if she's been around for a long time? Why would someone bring her to the doll hospital?"

Timothy said, "And why bring her to the kitchen door?"

"Maybe someone saw the lights on in here and got confused," suggested Titus. He didn't sound as if he thought this explained very much.

"But the lights are on upstairs, too," said Sarah-Jane. "Besides, my dad just made this beautiful new sign that says *Doll Hospital*. It points up the outside stairs. It would be almost impossible to miss it."

Timothy frowned. "Suppose someone *did* miss the sign and came to the back door instead. Why wouldn't that person wait until someone answered the door? You'd want to explain what was wrong, wouldn't you? You wouldn't just leave a valuable doll on the doorstep and run away!"

"Right," said Titus. "We don't even know who it belongs to."

Sarah-Jane didn't say anything.

She had another idea about the doll that she didn't even want to say out loud.

Maybe—just maybe—the doll was a present for her from a secret pal or something.

Maybe—just maybe—it was meant to be a

special addition to her doll collection.

Or maybe—just maybe—she was totally nuts.

Sarah-Jane took the beautiful doll back from Titus. She sighed and held her close.

"S-J," said Titus. "You're not getting attached to that doll, are you?"

"Definitely not," said Sarah-Jane, trying to sound offended that anyone would even think such a thing.

"Good," said Timothy. "Because knowing you, you've probably named her already."

"I most certainly have not," said Sarah-Jane.

She didn't tell them she had pretty much decided on *Sally Elizabeth.*

"Well," said Titus. "We were going to go say hi to Spider anyway. We should take the doll upstairs and see what he and Aunt Sue think about it."

"Good idea," agreed Timothy.

It was the *only* idea, really. So Sarah-Jane didn't argue with them.

She hugged Sally Elizabeth with one hand and picked up the basket with the other.

That's when a little piece of paper fluttered to the floor.

5

The Mysterious Note

Sarah-Jane's hands were full, so the boys pounced on the paper.

At the top of the paper, there was a little blotch of blue, like a design that had been partly torn away.

Something passed through Sarah-Jane's mind. Just a little whisper of something familiar. She thought she recognized the design from somewhere. But she couldn't remember where. And she couldn't even tell what the design was.

Anyway, she didn't have time to think about it, because there was writing on the paper.

Just three hastily printed words:

Please help me!

"OKaaay . . ." said Titus carefully.

"Things are getting seriously weird here," declared Timothy. "We get this *urgent* note. But it doesn't tell us what it wants us to do. What does it mean?"

Sarah-Jane said, "I don't know. But Sally Elizabeth is in some kind of trouble, and we have to help her!"

"Sally Elizabeth?" asked Titus, sounding thoroughly confused. "Who's Sally Elizabeth?"

Sarah-Jane bit her lip. She hadn't meant to let that slip out. But the note had flustered her.

"It's the *doll*!" cried Timothy. "You *named* her, didn't you? I *knew* it!"

"So what if I did?" replied Sarah-Jane. "Everybody needs a name, right? The point is, Sally Elizabeth also needs our help!"

Timothy and Titus looked at each other and shook their heads. Sometimes it just didn't pay to argue.

6

The Doll Hospital

Mrs. Cooper and Spider had a rule: At the doll hospital, kids came first.

Spider usually fixed dolls in the order they came in. And with so many grown-ups bringing old dolls in for repair, it could take Spider a while to get to all of them. People understood that their dolls would have to wait their turn.

But if a *kid* came in with a broken doll, that doll took cuts and went to the head of the line. Mrs. Cooper said that's because kids' dolls were so important to them. It would be too hard on kids to wait a long time to get their precious dolls back.

Spider called this the "emergency room" of the doll hospital.

The doll hospital was one part of a huge

office-workroom that took up the entire attic of the house.

Sarah-Jane, Timothy, and Titus took the inside stairs up to the workroom. They were bursting with news about their mysterious bundle.

But they had to stand back and wait.

Mrs. Cooper was going over fabric samples with a customer.

And Spider was talking to a little girl and her grandmother.

The little girl's lip trembled and a tear ran down her face as she held out her doll to Spider.

"There, there," said Spider gently. "Don't cry. It's not so bad."

"Not so bad?" muttered Titus under his breath. "That little dolly looks like it's been in a train wreck."

"Or the blender," murmured Timothy. "What on earth did she *do* to it?"

"She just *loved* it," whispered Sarah-Jane indignantly. "A *lot*."

"With friends like that . . ." said Titus.

". . . who needs enemies?" said Timothy.

"Ha!" said Sarah-Jane.

Sarah-Jane had her own little corner of the workroom where she could read or do homework or just hang out. The cousins went over there now and plopped down on floor cushions to wait.

The customers all left at the same time, so Mrs. Cooper and Spider were both free.

In Sarah-Jane's opinion, Spider could be kind of stern looking. Until he smiled. Then his whole face lit up, and he looked like the sweetest person in the world. Which he was.

He smiled at them now. "Hi, guys! What's up?"

It took a while—quite a while—to explain about the knock on the kitchen door, and the foundling, and the mysterious note.

When they were done, neither Mrs. Cooper nor Spider knew what to make of it at all.

"That's it?" asked Sarah-Jane's mother. "Just this little note?"

Sarah-Jane did what she figured she should have thought of before. She unwrapped the blanket all the way and shook it out. Nothing fell on the floor. Then she ran her fingers around the inside and outside of the basket. Nothing there, either.

Spider read the note aloud. " 'Please help me!' Help with what, I wonder? There's nothing wrong with this doll as far as I can see."

"That's what we thought, too," said Titus.

"In fact, it's in almost perfect condition," said Spider, examining the doll more carefully. "The back seam looks as if it's been undone and stitched up again at some point. But that doesn't matter. This doll is just wonderful! A real piece of American folk art. I'm surprised it's not in a museum."

"It's so odd the way it just turned up here,"

said Sarah-Jane's mother.

Spider nodded. "And—come to think of it—that's the second odd thing that's happened today."

7

The Second Odd Thing

*T*itus said, "Well—now that you have our undivided attention . . ."

Spider laughed. "It's probably nothing."

He said to Mrs. Cooper, "Did you notice that guy who came in here just a little while ago?"

"Vaguely," said Sarah-Jane's mother. "I was busy with Mrs. Stewart and her fabric samples. What did he look like?"

Spider shook his head. "To tell you the truth, I didn't really notice a whole lot. Bald. Tan jacket. Medium height. A little plump, maybe?"

He looked apologetically at the cousins. "I'm not much of a detective, I'm afraid."

The cousins told him not to worry about it.

Timothy said, "But if this guy was so ordinary looking, then why did you say he was odd?"

"Well, it's just that he came in here asking to buy a doll," said Spider. "And I explained that we don't *sell* dolls, we just *fix* them. But he didn't leave. He just kept looking at the shelves as if he was—I don't know—*searching* for something. It was a little irritating, actually. So I explained again that those dolls aren't for sale. That they all belonged to people. Finally, he just left without another word."

"What shelves?" asked Timothy, looking around the workroom.

"Come on, I'll show you," said Spider. He led them to his work space and pulled back a floor-to-ceiling curtain.

Behind the curtain were rows and rows of shelves.

And on the shelves were dozens of dolls— some in desperate need of repair.

Not a pretty sight.

And in addition to the dolls were all the parts for repairing them. Heads without bodies. Bodies without heads. Arms. Legs. Wigs. Even boxes of glass eyes.

Sarah-Jane had gotten used to this, but it had taken a little while. So it was nice to hear Timothy and Titus gasp.

"OK," said Titus. "Now, *this* is odd."

"Gross," said Timothy. "It looks like some kind of horror movie."

Spider laughed. "No argument there. In fact, that's why we put the curtain up. Little kids think their dolls are almost human. So we figured it would be too upsetting for them to see—well, to see all this." He waved his arm at the shelves.

Titus said, "But the curtains were open when that guy came up?"

Spider nodded. "Exactly. I leave them open when I'm working because it's easier to reach my supplies. I just close them when I hear a little kid coming up the stairs."

"Huh," said Timothy. "I wonder what the guy wanted."

"It's odd, all right," said Titus.

Sarah-Jane had been quiet through this whole discussion. Now she said, "I'll tell you what's odd. That guy was probably up here about the same time someone was knocking on the kitchen door."

8

Footprints

*T*hey were all quiet for a minute, just thinking about this. Two odd things happening at about the same time.

"Do you think there's a connection?" asked Spider.

"Could be," said Timothy. "Just because we can't see the connection doesn't mean it's not there."

"Or it could just be a coincidence," said Titus. He didn't sound as if he believed this, though.

Sarah-Jane didn't think it was a coincidence, either.

"Well," said Spider. "Maybe I need to call my girlfriend and tell her I'll be working late."

He picked up the doll the little girl had

brought in, and they couldn't help laughing.

Just then a young couple came in to see Sarah-Jane's mother about slipcovers.

So the cousins figured it was time to make themselves scarce.

Sarah-Jane left Sally Elizabeth with Spider. (Even though Timothy and Titus had to practically pry her fingers off the doll's basket!)

"Now what?" asked Timothy when they were back downstairs.

They all had that uncomfortable feeling you get when you know there's unfinished business but you don't know what to do about it.

Just sitting around waiting for the doll's owner to come back didn't sound that great.

"Well," said Sarah-Jane. "We could go outside and look around by the kitchen door for clues. I mean, we all got so interested in Sally Elizabeth that we didn't do that before."

Timothy and Titus wouldn't admit that they had gotten interested in Sally Elizabeth. But they did admit that they hadn't looked very hard for clues.

So the detective cousins got their coats and went outside.

Detective work can be hard and even a little boring. You can look and look and look and not find anything.

That didn't happen this time.

This time they got lucky.

The first clue they found was right under their noses as soon as they opened the kitchen door.

They hadn't noticed it before because they had been so surprised to see the foundling there.

But now they noticed a little clump of dirt. It looked as if it could have come from someone's shoes.

"OK," said Titus. "It looks like someone stepped in mud. Probably the same person who left the doll."

"Which means there should be footprints in the mud somewhere," said Timothy, looking around the yard.

"What mud?" asked Sarah-Jane, also looking around.

It was a fair question.

Unfortunately, no one had an answer for it. The grass was a little damp, maybe. But there were no big patches of mud that the cousins could see.

Sarah-Jane said, "Even if there were lots of mud on the ground, why would you have to step in it? Why not just stay on the sidewalk?"

Another fair question.

Suddenly Sarah-Jane pointed and said, "There's some mud on the ground over there."

Timothy and Titus looked at her in surprise. She was pointing at an evergreen bush.

It was one of Sarah-Jane's favorite spots in the whole yard. She loved to sit under it taking long, deep breaths, trying to fill up to the brim with the scent of evergreen.

"It may not be an *excellent* hiding place," said Sarah-Jane. "But it would be good enough in a pinch. After all, we didn't see anyone when we opened the door and took a look around."

"A *quick* look," said Timothy.

"That's true," agreed Sarah-Jane. She didn't like the idea of anything getting past them any more than he did.

Titus said, "We don't know for sure that anyone was hiding, but it fits. If it was kids playing a joke, they'd want to hang around to see what happened."

"And you can see the kitchen door from there," said Sarah-Jane.

Without another word, the cousins went over to the bush and examined the ground around it.

"Footprints!" cried Sarah-Jane. She figured there had to be. But it was still nice to find proof you were right.

"Only one set of footprints," said Timothy.

Titus said, "The shape is strange. The toe is kind of pointy and the heel is so small."

"High-heeled shoes," said Sarah-Jane with

authority. "Or boots, maybe."

The cousins looked at one another.

A grown-up lady?

Banging on the kitchen door?

Leaving a mysterious bundle on the door-step?

And hiding behind an evergreen bush?

"Well," said Titus. "I think that just about clears everything up."

He was kidding, of course.

9

More Clues

Now that the cousins knew someone had hidden behind the bush, they could see the tracks across the grass.

But that didn't make things any easier to understand.

That was because it looked as if the lady had gone from the sidewalk across the grass to the bush.

Then from the bush to the kitchen door.

Then from the kitchen door back to the bush.

Then from the bush back to the sidewalk.

What on earth was going on here?

The cousins took a closer look around the bush.

And that's when they found two more clues.

The first was a dark brown button.

The second was a little slip of paper.

On the slip of paper, there was a little blue blotch.

It was torn at the top, so it didn't look like much of anything.

But it was enough to make Sarah-Jane gasp.

"What? What?" asked Timothy and Titus together.

Sarah-Jane whipped the note out of her pocket and put it together with the slip they had just found. One piece on the left. The other piece on the right. The pieces fit together like a jigsaw puzzle. They didn't show the whole picture of anything. But that didn't stop Sarah-Jane from crying, "Aha! I *knew* it!"

Timothy and Titus looked at each other. "Knew what?" they asked.

"I knew that the little bit of blue blotch on the first slip of paper reminded me of something. Only I didn't know what. But now we have another blotch. And now it all makes sense!"

"S-J!" exclaimed Titus. "It's not making any sense at all!"

"Look at the blotches together," said Sarah-Jane. "What do you see?"

"OK," said Timothy. "If I put the blotches together and look very, *very* hard, it looks like . . . like . . . the bottom half of a kangaroo."

"Yes!" cried Sarah-Jane. "Exactly!"

10

The Blue Kangaroo

The boys stared at her.

Sarah-Jane had seen that look once already today. The one that meant: Our cousin has lost her mind.

"Oh, for crying out loud," said Sarah-Jane. "What *color* is the kangaroo?"

"Blue," said Titus carefully, as if he knew the right answer but had no idea what it meant. "It's a *blue* kangaroo."

"Right!" said Sarah-Jane, as if this explained everything. "It's *The Blue Kangaroo*! Honestly! Sometimes it's so hard to get through to you people!"

"The Blue Kangaroo," muttered Timothy. "Why does that sound familiar to me?"

"Because you've walked right by there a

zillion times," said Sarah-Jane. "It's a *store*. You *know*! The one that sells all that adorable baby stuff."

"Ohhhhh," said Timothy and Titus together as they finally saw what she was getting to. "*That* place."

The little country town of Fairfield, where Sarah-Jane lived, was known for its beautiful old houses and its quaint little shops.

Timothy and Titus were not fans of quaint little shops.

"Right," said Sarah-Jane. "And this drawing is their logo. You know, a *logo* is the little picture that stands for a store or a company."

"Right," said Titus. "Companies print it on their stationery. They put it on boxes and bags. That kind of thing."

"Exactly," said Sarah-Jane.

"So what are we saying?" asked Timothy. "That the lady who hid behind the evergreen bush is someone who shops at The Blue Kangaroo?"

"Or someone who works there," said Sarah-Jane. "At least it's a start."

Timothy and Titus looked at her uneasily.

Sarah-Jane could tell they didn't like the sound of this.

"Well, obviously," said Sarah-Jane. "We have to go hang around The Blue Kangaroo and see what we can find out. We can pretend we're shopping for a baby shower gift or something."

Actually, this didn't strike Sarah-Jane as that great of a cover story. But it was all she could come up with at the moment, and she didn't want to share her doubts. Timothy and Titus were looking pretty doubtful as it was.

"Hang around a little store that sells adorable baby stuff?" said Titus. "I don't *think* so."

"First it's a doll hospital, and now this," said Timothy. "No way. Uh-uh."

"You guys!" cried Sarah-Jane. "Don't you want to find out what's going on? What kind of detectives are you?"

Timothy and Titus looked at each other and groaned.

Sarah-Jane knew she had them.

"Oh, all right, we'll go," said Timothy. "But that doesn't mean we have to like it."

Titus said, "We're only hanging around a cute little store because sometimes a man's gotta do what a man's gotta do."

"Whatever," said Sarah-Jane.

11

More Detective Work

Whenever the cousins visited one another, they brought their bikes along. You never knew when you would need wheels. Sarah-Jane was just about to tell her mother they were going out, when the phone rang. It was Sarah-Jane's mother calling, telling them to come upstairs.

Sarah-Jane gulped back a groan.

She did messenger work for her mother, and usually she liked this very much.

But now it meant the detective work would have to wait.

So frustrating!

Timothy and Titus were good sports about it. (They always helped her out with her errands when they were visiting.)

Today they were *especially* good sports

about it. Doing errands meant they wouldn't have to visit an adorable baby store.

"OK," said Sarah-Jane's mother, sounding a little rushed. "Three things:

"First, we're going to have to work through lunch, so I'd like you to pick up some sandwiches at the deli.

"Second, Mrs. Stewart left her tote bag, so I need you to take that over to her house. Here's the address.

"And third, Marilyn didn't come by to pick up this box of baby clothes I just finished. It needs to go to The Blue Kangaroo. Can you take it there for me?"

"No problem," said Sarah-Jane calmly.

She didn't look at her cousins.

She knew they were probably falling on the floor.

Sarah-Jane waited until they got outside to say, "Yippee! Now we don't need a cover story to go in The Blue Kangaroo. Isn't this *fantastic*?"

"Marvelous," said Timothy.

"Fabulous," said Titus.

"Well, it *is*," said Sarah-Jane. "We need to find out what's going on." (Her mother had

47

been so busy the cousins hadn't even *tried* to explain about a lady from The Blue Kangaroo hiding behind their evergreen bush!)

So now the three detective cousins took off to see what they could find out.

They dropped the tote bag off first. And they figured they could pick up the sandwiches last.

But for now the most important thing was the baby store.

Even Timothy and Titus were looking pretty interested.

But if the cousins expected everything to make sense as soon as they walked through the door, they were sadly mistaken.

For one thing, the lady behind the counter didn't look startled to see them. She didn't look as if she'd been banging on their kitchen door and hiding behind their evergreen bush.

For another thing, she was wearing flat shoes. (The cousins had ambled by the counter to take a look without seeming to look at anything.)

But on the plus side, they noticed a little note pad on the counter. With the logo of a blue kangaroo.

One out of three wasn't bad.

It was hard not to jump up and down and give themselves high fives. But that didn't seem like something detectives should do.

The lady finished with a customer and smiled at them. "Can I help you?" she asked.

"Yes," said Sarah-Jane. "I'm Sue Cooper's daughter, and she sent me with some baby clothes."

"Oh, yes!" exclaimed the woman, whose name tag said *Chris*. "I've been *dying* to see them. Your mother does such *exquisite* work! Marilyn was supposed to pick the clothes up for me, but she said they weren't ready yet."

The cousins looked at one another in surprise. According to Sarah-Jane's mother, Marilyn had never showed up.

12

The T.C.D.C.

"Who's Marilyn?" asked Sarah-Jane. "Does she work here?"

"Part time," said Chris. "She does the windows and the store decorations."

"Is she working today?" asked Timothy.

"Yes," said Chris, looking a little surprised at the question. "She came in a little while ago. But she just stepped next door to pick up some sandwiches. Why do you ask?"

"Could I use the washroom?" asked Sarah-Jane before Timothy had to answer.

"Sure," said Chris. "It's just back there to the left of the office."

It hadn't been a fib. Sarah-Jane really did have to use the washroom. But she also wanted to take a look at a brown coat she saw hanging in the back room.

It was just as Sarah-Jane suspected. The coat was missing a button.

Sarah-Jane slipped the brown button they had found out of her pocket and held it up to the other buttons on the coat.

A perfect match.

Just then the little bell over the front door jangled as someone came in.

"Oh," said Chris. "Here's Marilyn now."

Unlike Chris, Marilyn *was* startled to see them.

Very.

Sarah-Jane got right to the point. "We came to ask you about the doll," she said.

In her heart of hearts, Sarah-Jane hoped that Marilyn would say, "Why, my dear! I left the doll outside your kitchen door as a secret present for you!"

But, of course, she didn't.

Instead, Marilyn gasped. "I was sure no one had seen me!"

"We didn't see you," said Timothy.

"Then how did you know?"

"This and that," said Titus. "Your footprints, for one thing."

Everyone glanced at Marilyn's boots, which were still a little muddy.

"Then there was the button you lost," said Sarah-Jane. "That's your brown coat back there. Right?"

Marilyn nodded. "I didn't need it just to run next door."

Timothy picked up the note pad from the counter. He said, "I'm guessing you have a little note pad like this. The note that said *Please help me!* was written on paper from The Blue Kangaroo."

"'*Please help me*'?" said Chris. "Marilyn, what's the matter? What's going on?"

Marilyn glanced at the cousins.

"We have no idea what's going on," said Timothy. "The T.C.D.C. can figure out some clues, but you have to tell us the rest."

"What's a 'teesy-deesy'?" asked Marilyn and Chris together.

"It's letters," explained Sarah-Jane. "Capital T. Capital C. Capital D. Capital C. It stands for the Three Cousins Detective Club. I'm Sarah-Jane Cooper, and these are my cousins Timothy Dawson and Titus McKay."

Marilyn sighed. "Leaving the doll on the doorstep with that note was a crazy thing to do. But I panicked."

"Panicked?" asked Titus. "Why?"

Marilyn sighed again. "Because the doll was stolen. I mean, *I* stole it."

13

A Strange Story

The cousins tried not to gasp. But they couldn't help it. This was the last thing they expected to hear.

"Start at the beginning," said Chris gently. Marilyn took a deep breath.

She said, "Because of my store decorating job, I'm always looking for interesting ways to display things. I go to garage sales and flea markets and auctions to find things I can use."

She waved a hand around the store. The cousins saw new baby blankets draped across an antique cradle and bibs piled on an old high chair. They nodded.

Marilyn continued. "Recently I got to go through an old house in preparation for an estate sale. A nephew had inherited everything from his elderly aunt.

"Well, his aunt was a friend of mine, the dearest old lady. And she used to tell me this strange story."

The cousins had already been listening closely. But now their ears *really* perked up! Any story is interesting. A "strange story" is irresistible.

"The story was about a doll my friend once had," said Marilyn. "A beautiful doll that her mother had made for her."

"Sally Elizabeth!" cried Sarah-Jane.

Marilyn looked confused. "Who's Sally Elizabeth?" she asked.

Sarah-Jane felt her face grow hot. "I . . . um . . . sort of named her," she mumbled.

Marilyn smiled. "So did I. I thought she looked like a Caroline. But my friend referred to her as Arabella."

Sarah-Jane nodded. She could live with either of those.

"So what's the strange part of the story?" asked Timothy, who clearly felt they were wandering from the point.

"The strange part," said Marilyn, "is that

my friend's father supposedly had some jewels. I don't know where they came from or what he planned to do with them. But he had the odd idea that the best place to hide them would be inside a child's doll. No one would ever think of looking for them there."

The cousins thought about this for a moment. It did sound odd, but as hiding places went, it wasn't bad.

Marilyn went on, "My friend always said the doll—with the jewels still inside her—was still in the house. But she couldn't remember where.

"To tell you the truth, I thought it was an interesting story. No more than that. My friend's mind wandered sometimes. And she would get agitated.

"One of the things that worried her was that her nephew would just rip open the doll to get the jewels."

Sarah-Jane gave a little cry of horror.

Marilyn nodded. "My feelings exactly! And that was even before I found the doll. I didn't even know what I had at first, because it was wrapped in a blanket and tucked in a basket. I guess my friend used it as a doll's cradle when she was little. I fell in love with that doll at first sight. She was in perfect condition. And I knew I couldn't let anything happen to her."

Marilyn paused, looking very embarrassed.

"The point is, I sneaked the doll out of the house. I know now that I should have tried talking to my friend's nephew. But I was afraid he would just grab the doll and run. Then what could I do? It was his doll. But she belongs in a museum."

Sarah-Jane nodded. "That's what Spider says. He also says the doll had been opened up and restitched. So maybe the strange story is true."

"Speaking of Spider . . ." said Titus.

Marilyn nodded. "My plan was to take Caroline to the doll hospital and see if Spider could open her up without damaging her to see if there are any jewels hidden inside. If there are, then of course they would go to my friend's nephew. Which is probably all he cares about. And the doll could go to a museum."

"Sounds like a good plan," said Timothy. "Not the stealing part. But taking the doll to Spider."

"So what happened?" asked Titus.

14

Hide-and-Seek

Marilyn shook her head as if she couldn't quite believe what had happened.

She said, "I was supposed to pick up some baby clothes anyway. So I brought the doll along. I was nervous enough about having something that didn't belong to me! But when I got there, who should I see but my friend's nephew!"

"Bald guy?" asked Timothy. "Kind of plump? Wears a tan jacket?"

Marilyn stared at them, flabbergasted. "You kids are amazing!"

The cousins shrugged. What could they say? Sometimes they amazed themselves.

"So you saw the nephew . . ." prompted Sarah-Jane.

"Yes," said Marilyn. "When he couldn't find the doll, he must have suspected that I had it. And if you wanted to get something out of a doll, a doll hospital would be a good place to take it.

"Anyway, I saw him, and—this is so silly—I ducked behind a bush.

"You can see both the workroom and the kitchen from there. I saw you kids inside the kitchen. That's when I got the idea of leaving the doll with you. I was just so panicky about getting caught with it."

"So why didn't you go up and talk to Spider after the guy left?" asked Timothy reasonably.

"I was going to," said Marilyn. "But who should I see going up to the workroom but my mother and my little niece."

It took the cousins a moment to process this.

Titus said, "You mean the little girl with the train-wreck doll is your niece?"

Marilyn laughed. "If it's the doll I'm thinking of, I gave it to her when she was born. She never lets it out of her sight."

"Spider's working on it now," said Sarah-

Jane. "So you didn't want your mother and niece to see you?"

Marilyn nodded. "I knew my mother would know something was up, and I didn't want to explain about stealing the doll."

Again the cousins were quiet, thinking about this. It seemed that no matter how old you got, there were certain things you didn't want to have to tell your mother.

"Besides," said Marilyn. "I didn't want my niece even to hear about the doll. If she got one look at her, she would fall in love with her. And that would be too hard when she couldn't have her."

Sarah-Jane nodded. Been there. Done that.

"It was such a foolish game of hide-and-seek I was playing," said Marilyn. "I just wanted to get out of there until I could figure out what to do."

"And have you?" asked Sarah-Jane. "Figured out what to do, I mean?"

"Yes," said Marilyn. "I know exactly what I have to do."

15

The Doll's Surprise

Marilyn called her friend's nephew and asked him to meet her at the doll hospital.

The cousins rode over on their bikes and met them there. (They figured they could always come back for the sandwiches later.)

Spider was not too happy about opening up the beautiful doll. If it had been up to him, he would have left it alone. Jewels or no jewels.

But there didn't seem to be any choice. And no one could do the job better than Spider.

Carefully, carefully, he undid the old stitching. Gently, gently, he removed the stuffing.

It took a long time, and it was like watching an operation.

Sarah-Jane only hoped she wouldn't faint.

When the stuffing was spread out on the table, the nephew picked through it.

And came up with a small bag.

Filled with diamonds.

The strange story was true.

Once he had the diamonds, the man was happy to sign the doll over to Marilyn.

As soon as the man was gone, Spider began putting the doll back together again. Soon she would be as good as new.

Marilyn called the Fairfield Museum from the workroom. She described the doll as a marvelous piece of folk art. And the cousins could tell from her face that the museum people were as excited as she was.

"What's that?" asked Marilyn into the phone. "Oh, yes." (Here she winked at Sarah-Jane.) "The doll's name is Sally Elizabeth."

The End

Series for Young Readers*
From Bethany House Publishers

★ ★ ★

The Adventures of Callie Ann
by Shannon Mason Leppard
Readers will giggle their way through the true-to-life escapades of Callie Ann Davies and her many North Carolina friends.

★ ★ ★

Backpack Mysteries
by Mary Carpenter Reid
This excitement-filled mystery series follows the mishaps and adventures of Steff and Paulie Larson as they strive to help often-eccentric relatives crack their toughest cases.

★ ★ ★

The Cul-de-sac Kids
by Beverly Lewis
Each story in this lighthearted series features the hilarious antics and predicaments of nine endearing boys and girls who live on Blossom Hill Lane.

★ ★ ★

Ruby Slippers School
by Stacy Towle Morgan
Join the fun as home-schoolers Hope and Annie Brown visit fascinating countries and meet inspiring Christians from around the world!

★ ★ ★

Three Cousins Detective Club®
by Elspeth Campbell Murphy
Famous detective cousins Timothy, Titus, and Sarah-Jane learn compelling Scripture-based truths while finding—and solving—intriguing mysteries.

* (ages 7–10)

9611